Quantum Horizons: Conversations at the Edge of Discovery

Sayeda Subha Ashrafy Shifa

Ukiyoto Publishing

All global publishing rights are held by

Ukiyoto Publishing

Published in 2024

Content Copyright © Sayeda Subha Ashrafy Shifa

ISBN 9789361724039

All rights reserved.

No part of this publication may be reproduced, transmitted, or stored in a retrieval system, in any form by any means, electronic, mechanical, photocopying, recording or otherwise, without the prior permission of the publisher.

The moral rights of the author have been asserted.

This is a work of fiction. Names, characters, businesses, places, events, locales, and incidents are either the products of the author's imagination or used in a fictitious manner. Any resemblance to actual persons, living or dead, or actual events is purely coincidental.

This book is sold subject to the condition that it shall not by way of trade or otherwise, be lent, resold, hired out or otherwise circulated, without the publisher's prior consent, in any form of binding or cover other than that in which it is published.

www.ukiyoto.com

Okay, So the list is huge:
Sidratul Muntaha Priya
Abdus Samiul Basir Prangon
Ananna Rashid Bhuiyan
Tamanna Bhuiyan Senjuty
Siam Tahsin Bhuiyan
Sayed Abrar Habib Shifty
Tasnim Bhuiyan Shuddhity
Sauda Akhanda
Sayed Anjum Habib Shafin
Raita Akhanda
Masrur Aswad Bhuiyan Pridim
Sarah Tabassum Bhuiyan
Rufaida Rashid Bhuiyan
Shahrima Jannat oishwee
Rhyan Jannat Esha
Rubaia Afroz Swati

Thanks to all my lovely brothers and sisters and,
Abid Hossain Romat (my best friend)

Synopsis:

In the unfolding chapters of "Quantum Horizons," Dr. Emily Morgan and her team embark on an intellectual odyssey that transcends the conventional boundaries of scientific exploration. Their conversations, infused with intellectual vigor and shared passion, not only push the limits of quantum theory but also delve into the societal, ethical, and philosophical dimensions of their groundbreaking discoveries.

As the quantum revolution gains momentum, the team's discussions evolve into a symphony of innovation and responsibility. The narrative explores the potential of quantum technologies not just as scientific marvels but as instruments that could reshape the very fabric of human existence. The team contemplates how quantum computing might revolutionize industries, heralding a new era of computational power that transforms problem-solving and decision-making across diverse fields.

Ethical considerations become a guiding compass for Dr. Morgan's team. The narrative navigates through the ethical landscape of quantum advancements, addressing concerns of access, fairness, and the responsible integration of these technologies into everyday life. The team grapples with the responsibility that comes with pushing the boundaries of knowledge, aiming for a future where the benefits of quantum technologies are equitably distributed and contribute to the betterment of society as a whole.

The exploration of quantum communication, anchored by the mind-bending concept of entanglement, adds a layer of intrigue to the narrative. The team envisions a future where secure and instantaneous communication can transcend geographical distances, sparking discussions not just on the technical aspects but also on the societal impact of such advancements. They contemplate how a globally connected quantum network could reshape the way humanity communicates, opening new possibilities for collaboration and

understanding.

As the narrative unfolds, the team's intellectual curiosity extends beyond the scientific realm into the metaphysical. Conversations delve into the nature of reality itself, the potential existence of multi-dimensional quantum computing, and the profound philosophical implications of quantum mechanics. These dialogues with artists, writers, and visionaries provide a holistic perspective on the beauty and complexity of the quantum world, emphasizing the interconnectedness of science and creativity.

The climax of "Quantum Horizons" is not just a conclusion but a transition to the next phase of exploration. Dr. Morgan's team, inspired by their discoveries and the power of conversations, steps into uncharted territories with a renewed sense of purpose. The narrative leaves readers with a sense of anticipation, echoing the sentiment that the journey into quantum horizons has only scratched the surface of what lies ahead. A story about ethics, emotion, science, thrilling, action, all in one you can think.

In "Quantum Horizons," the narrative unfolds as a tapestry where scientific curiosity, ethical considerations, and philosophical reflections are interwoven seamlessly. It serves as an intellectual and emotional journey, inviting readers to contemplate the implications of quantum advancements and the profound impact that responsible exploration can have on the future of humanity. The story stands not just as a chronicle of scientific discovery but as an ode to the limitless possibilities that emerge when curiosity and responsibility walk hand in hand towards the quantum horizons of tomorrow.

Contents

The Mysterious Experiment	1
The Quantum Puzzle	4
The Ethical Dilemma	8
Unveiling the Quantum Revolution	11
Exploring the Quantum Frontiers	15
The Ethics of Quantum Power	19
Quantum Security and the Battle for Encryption	23
Quantum Society and Ethical Integration	27
Quantum Communication and the Era of Secure Connectivity	31
The Quantum Frontier - Exploring the Unknown	35
About the Author	*39*

The Mysterious Experiment

Dr. Emily Morgan sat in her lab, eagerly observing the complex quantum experiment she had been working on for months. Excitement filled the air as her team, consisting of Dr. Mark Turner and Dr. Sarah Parker, prepared to witness a groundbreaking event in the realm of quantum physics.

The experiment involved a sophisticated setup of particle accelerators, quantum entanglement generators, and detectors. Emily had dedicated her career to unraveling the mysteries of quantum mechanics, and this experiment promised to deliver a breakthrough that could revolutionize the field.

As the experiment commenced, a hush fell over the lab. The particle accelerators whirred to life, propelling atoms to collide at incredible speeds. The quantum entanglement generators synchronized, entangling the particles in a web of interconnectedness. All eyes were fixed on the detectors, waiting for the moment of revelation.

Suddenly, a strange phenomenon unfolded before their eyes. The particles, instead of behaving according to the predictable patterns of classical physics, exhibited inexplicable behavior. They seemed to defy the laws that govern the macrosco pic world. Emily's excitement quickly turned into astonishment and bewilderment.

The detectors registered peculiar readings—patterns of interference that had never been observed before. The entangled particles appeared to communicate instantaneously, regardless of distance, as if connected by an invisible thread. The implications of this discovery were staggering.

Emily couldn't contain her amazement. "We've stumbled upon something truly extraordinary," she exclaimed. The experiment had unveiled a potential breakthrough in the understanding of quantum entanglement and its ramifications for the fundamental nature of reality.

However, the elation within the lab soon gave way to a sense of urgency. The team realized that their discovery demanded further investigation and analysis. They needed to understand the underlying mechanisms behind this unprecedented behavior and ascertain the practical implications it held.

Emily, Mark, and Sarah gathered around a whiteboard, fervently sketching diagrams and scribbling equations. They sought to comprehend how the entangled particles had managed to communicate instantaneously, surpassing the limitations imposed by the speed of light.

Hours turned into days as they delved deeper into the intricacies of quantum entanglement. They poured over scientific papers, consulted renowned experts in the field, and conducted additional experiments to validate their initial findings.

The more they learned, the more fascinated and perplexed they became. Quantum entanglement, once a topic of theoretical conjecture and conjecture, was now tangible evidence of a new frontier in science. It held the promise of teleportation, secure communication, and seemingly impossible technological advancements.

Emily was filled with a renewed sense of purpose. She was determined to harness this newfound knowledge for the betterment of humanity. But she was also cognizant of the ethical implications that lay before her and her team. Their breakthrough had the potential to reshape the world, and they needed to tread cautiously.

With a deep breath, Emily addressed her team. "We have embarked upon a journey that will challenge our understanding of the fabric of reality. It is our responsibility to ensure that our discoveries bring positive change while minimizing the risks involved. Let us proceed with prudence and integrity."

The team nodded in agreement, acknowledging the weight of their aspirations. They understood that their path would not be easy. They would face skepticism, obstacles, and perhaps even unintended consequences. But they were driven by a shared curiosity and a collective belief in the power of scientific progress.

The Quantum Puzzle

Driven by their insatiable curiosity, Dr. Emily Morgan and her team immersed themselves in a world of quantum mechanics. Their groundbreaking experiment had revealed a remarkable phenomenon: particles entangled in a web of interconnectedness that allowed for instantaneous communication. Now, they needed to understand the underlying principles behind this perplexing behavior.

Emily pored over scientific journals, scrutinizing the works of past and contemporary quantum physicists. It felt as if she had stepped into a labyrinth of complex theories and mathematical equations, each one offering a glimpse into the mysterious fabric of the quantum world.

As days turned into weeks, Emily's understanding deepened. She began to grasp the intricate concepts that seemed to defy intuition. Quantum entanglement, she realized, was not merely a strange occurrence but an inherent property of the quantum realm itself.

Driven by her newfound knowledge, Emily gathered her team in the lab once more. Equations and diagrams covered the whiteboard, displaying the interconnectedness of particles and the mathematical foundations of quantum entanglement. Emily sketched out her plan to delve even deeper into the phenomenon.

"We need to continue our experiments," Emily emphatically stated. "We must explore the limits of quantum entanglement and investigate how we can harness its power for technological advancements."

Mark and Sarah nodded in agreement, sharing Emily's enthusiasm. They had become captivated by the potential of quantum entanglement and its implications for the future of science. With a renewed sense of purpose, they set out to design a series of experiments that would push the boundaries of their understanding.

The team reconfigured the setup in their lab, incorporating more precise detectors and advanced quantum entanglement generators. They meticulously calibrated their instruments and prepared for the next phase of their investigation.

As they conducted their experiments, they encountered both success and challenges. They observed entangled particles behaving in ways they could not have anticipated. Quantum entanglement defied conventional notions of cause and effect, presenting a realm where probability and possibility intertwined.

Amidst their progress, Emily's team found themselves faced with profound questions. How could they ensure the stability of entanglement over long distances? Could they control the entanglement of particles for specific purposes? And what were the ethical considerations of manipulating entanglement for scientific progress?

In their search for answers, Emily and her team collaborated with prominent physicists around the world. They attended conferences, engaged in lively debates, and shared their findings. Through these conversations, they expanded their knowledge, refining their experiments and deepening their understanding of quantum entanglement.

But as they delved deeper into the quantum puzzle, they also encountered skepticism and opposition from some quarters. Established scientists dismissed their work as mere speculation, cautioning against the pursuit of what they saw as untested and potentially dangerous territory. Undeterred, Emily and her team believed in the significance of their discoveries and pressed onward.

One breakthrough followed another as the team built upon their previous experiments. They devised protocols to entangle particles over greater distances, extending the reach of their quantum connections. They also explored the potential of quantum entanglement for secure communication and encryption, envisioning a future where information could be transmitted instantaneously and securely across vast distances.

But the more they discovered, the more they realized the importance of ethical considerations. Emily understood that with great power came great responsibility. She was acutely aware of the potential dangers of misuse or unintended consequences that their research could bring. They were determined to pursue progress while upholding their moral and ethical principles.

The Ethical Dilemma

Dr. Emily Morgan and her team had made remarkable progress in their exploration of quantum entanglement. Their experiments had revealed new insights, expanded the boundaries of their understanding, and hinted at the immense potential of harnessing the power of entanglement for technological advancements. However, as they delved deeper into the mysteries of the quantum world, they found themselves facing complex ethical dilemmas.

The implications of their research were profound. The ability to entangle particles over vast distances opened doors to secure communication, supercomputing, and teleportation, among other possibilities. But Emily realized that with such immense power came great responsibility. They needed to consider the ethical consequences of their discoveries and the potential risks involved.

Gathered around the whiteboard once again, Emily, Mark, and Sarah engaged in a heated discussion. They grappled with questions that tested the very core of their morals and ethics. How would their research impact society? Could it inadvertently lead to devastating consequences in the wrong hands? What measures could they take to mitigate these risks?

It was clear to Emily that they couldn't proceed recklessly without considering the potential ramifications. She believed that the responsible pursuit of scientific progress required strict adherence to ethical principles. As they brainstorm possible solutions, they agreed to develop a comprehensive set of guidelines to govern their research and ensure it is aligned with their ethical values.

Their guidelines included principles such as transparency, accountability, and the application of the "do no harm" philosophy. They would commit to sharing their findings openly with the scientific community, engaging in peer review, and promoting responsible dialogue regarding the potential applications of their research. They also recognized that they had a duty to educate the public on the benefits and risks of quantum entanglement.

As they drafted their guidelines, Emily's team reached out to ethicists and legal experts, seeking their insights on the ethical dilemmas they faced. They organized interdisciplinary workshops, fostering discussions on the potential societal impacts of their research. Through these collaborations, they gained a broader understanding of the ethical challenges that arose from their work.

The team also engaged in rigorous self-reflection, constantly questioning their motivations and ensuring that their intentions aligned with the principles they had set forth. They recognized the importance of remaining vigilant and accountable for the potential consequences of their actions.

However, despite their diligent efforts, Emily's team faced criticism from certain quarters. Skeptics argued that their research was too dangerous to pursue, that there was no way to guarantee it wouldn't fall into the wrong hands. Others voiced concerns about the unintended consequences that could result from meddling with the fundamental fabric of reality.

These criticisms were not dismissed lightly. Emily and her team understood the gravity of their research and the ethical tightrope they were walking. They engaged with their critics, opening channels of dialogue, and sought to address their concerns head-on.

As their experiments continued to yield groundbreaking results, they also formed partnerships with governmental and international organizations. They advocated for the establishment of ethical and regulatory frameworks surrounding quantum technologies, emphasizing the need for responsible development and utilization.

Unveiling the Quantum Revolution

Dr. Emily Morgan and her team had confronted the ethical dilemmas surrounding their research on quantum entanglement. Now, armed with guidelines and a firm commitment to responsible innovation, they were ready to reveal their discoveries to the world and initiate a quantum revolution.

The team had spent months refining their experiments and analyzing the data they had collected. Their findings were groundbreaking - they had successfully entangled particles over long distances and developed protocols for stable and controlled entanglement. This opened up a plethora of possibilities for quantum communication, cryptography, and computation.

As the team prepared for a major scientific conference, an air of excitement filled the lab. Their presentation would mark a turning point in the world of quantum science. Emily, Mark, and Sarah meticulously prepared their slides, ensuring that their audience would grasp the significance of their research.

The day arrived, and Emily took the stage, showcasing their journey from the initial experiment to their current breakthroughs. She explained the principles of quantum entanglement, its potential applications, and the ethical framework they had developed to guide their research.

The audience was captivated by Emily's presentation. Scientists from various disciplines, policymakers, and industry representatives witnessed the unveiling of a scientific revolution. Questions filled the room, centered not only around the scientific aspects but also the broader societal implications of their discoveries.

Emily's team engaged in enthusiastic discussions, sharing their expertise and addressing concerns. They underscored the importance of collaboration, emphasizing that the quantum revolution required interdisciplinary efforts to fully comprehend and harness its power.

Following the conference, inquiries and collaborations poured in from around the world. Scientific institutions sought partnerships, governments considered the regulatory implications, and industry leaders envisioned the commercial potential of quantum technologies.

Emily's team became ambassadors and advocates for the responsible development of quantum technologies. They participated in policy debates, engaged with regulatory bodies, and contributed to the establishment of ethical standards and best practices. Their commitment to transparency and public engagement shaped the discourse around quantum research, ensuring that society's interests remained at the forefront.

Soon, quantum communication networks began to take shape. Emily's team collaborated with telecommunications companies to implement secure quantum key distribution, protecting sensitive information from potential breaches. The ability to transmit data with inherent security was a game-changer in an increasingly interconnected world.

The promise of quantum computing also drew significant attention. Emily's team worked closely with computer scientists and engineers, collectively exploring the potential for quantum algorithms and advanced computing architectures. They were making strides in solving complex problems that were once thought to be insurmountable.

As the quantum revolution gained momentum, Emily and her team continued to champion the importance of ethical considerations. They stressed the need for responsible innovation, ensuring that the potential risks and unintended consequences were considered at every step.

Their commitment to education and public awareness remained unwavering. They held workshops, engaged with schools and universities, and popularized quantum science through accessible media. They recognized that a well-informed society was crucial for making informed decisions about the societal implications of quantum technologies.

People around the world were captivated by the possibilities. They marveled at the potential for quantum communication, the prospects of supercomputing, and the transformative impact on various fields such as medicine, materials science, and finance.

Yet, amidst the triumphs and transformative potential, Emily and her team remained vigilant. They knew that the path forward required ongoing vigilance and the steadfast application of their ethical principles. The quantum revolution was just beginning, and their responsibilities as pioneers demanded constant reflection and adaptation.

Emily and her team embraced their role as stewards of the quantum revolution. With each subsequent chapter, they would navigate the ever-changing landscape, striving to ensure that humanity reaped the benefits of this extraordinary scientific frontier while safeguarding against potential risks.

Exploring the Quantum Frontiers

As the quantum revolution continued to unfold, Dr. Emily Morgan and her team found themselves at the forefront of innovation, constantly exploring new frontiers in the realm of quantum science. Chapter 5 witnessed their journey as they engaged in thought-provoking conversations with fellow scientists, policymakers, and industry leaders, further pushing the boundaries of their understanding

One afternoon, Emily sat in her office, engrossed in an intricate paper on quantum teleportation. Lost in her thoughts, she hardly noticed when Mark walked in with a curious expression on his face.

"Emily, have you seen this research on quantum teleportation using black holes?" he exclaimed, handing Emily a printed paper.

Emily scanned the article, her excitement building. "This is fascinating, Mark! The idea of harnessing the enigmatic properties of black holes for teleportation is mind-boggling. We should reach out to the authors and discuss their findings."

Mark nodded, his eyes gleaming with anticipation. "I think these conversations could spur new avenues of research. Let's explore the possibilities."

In the following weeks, Emily and Mark engaged in dialogue with the authors and other quantum physicists intrigued by the concept of utilizing black holes for teleportation. They exchanged ideas, debated the feasibility of the proposal, and proposed experiments to test the theory.

One evening, as they discussed the research with Sarah over dinner, a question arose: What if quantum teleportation could be applied to space exploration? Could it revolutionize interstellar travel?

Sarah pondered the question, her eyes filled with wonder. "Imagine, Emily, if quantum teleportation could transport matter across vast cosmic distances. It could potentially herald a new era of space exploration, allowing us to reach distant galaxies and exoplanets in a fraction of the time."

The conversation ignited their imaginations, spurring discussions about the possibilities and ethical considerations surrounding quantum teleportation in space exploration. They reflected on the potential impact on extraterrestrial life, the preservation of scientific integrity, and the need for responsible exploration beyond our planet.

Eager to gain insights from experts in the field, Emily's team reached out to leading astrophysicists and space agencies. These conversations delved into the challenges of interstellar travel, the effects of quantum teleportation on biological matter, and whether it was even possible to achieve such feats.

One memorable conversation took place with Dr. Natalie Bennett, an astrophysicist renowned for her groundbreaking research on black holes.

"Quantum teleportation is a fascinating concept," Dr. Bennett mused. "However, the energy requirements and the preservation of quantum coherence over such vast distances pose significant challenges. We would need to develop novel techniques to maintain quantum entanglement and ensure the integrity of teleported objects."

Emily nodded, absorbing Dr. Bennett's insights. "So, you believe that while it may be possible theoretically, we still have a long way to go in terms of technological advancements to realize practical interstellar teleportation?"

Dr. Bennett smiled warmly. "Indeed. The possibilities are awe-inspiring, but we must be mindful of the scientific and ethical implications. It will require collaborative efforts across disciplines to unlock the secrets of the universe."

Buoyed by the conversations they had engaged in, Emily's team became even more determined to continue pushing the boundaries of quantum science. They recognized that conversations with experts and thought leaders were invaluable in shaping their research and understanding.

Each discussion brought forth new perspectives and challenged preconceived notions. Whether exploring the potential for quantum computing in climate modeling or considering the impact of quantum entanglement on biology, Emily's team sought out the experts, eager to engage in collaborative discourse.

These conversations not only fueled their passion but also opened doors to unexpected collaborations. They joined forces with scientists from diverse fields, exchanging knowledge and expertise, and blending quantum principles with biology, chemistry, and other disciplines.

As Chapter 5 progressed, Emily's team grew even more passionate about the importance of fostering dialogue and collaboration in the scientific community. They believed that the collective wisdom of a diverse range of voices was crucial in unlocking the full potential of the quantum revolution.

The quantum frontiers, they realized, were vast and ever-expanding. Through their conversations and collaborations, Emily and her team propelled themselves into the unknown, embracing the inherent curiosity and wonder that drove the scientific pursuit. And with each conversation, they edged closer to unraveling the grand mysteries of the quantum realm.

The Ethics of Quantum Power

In the sixth chapter of the quantum revolution, Dr. Emily Morgan and her team found themselves grappling with the profound ethical implications of their groundbreaking research. As the power of quantum technologies continued to grow, questions arose regarding their responsible deployment and potential consequences.

Emily sat in a dimly lit conference room, surrounded by her colleagues, as an esteemed panel of experts discussed the ethical considerations of quantum power. The room was filled with tension and deliberation, as they dove into the societal impact and potential risks associated with quantum technologies.

One of the panelists, Dr. Sofia Ramirez, a renowned expert in bioethics, raised a critical concern. "As we delve deeper into the applications of quantum technologies, we must not overlook the potential for misuse and unintended consequences. How do we ensure that these technologies are used responsibly, without harming individuals or infringing on privacy?"

Emily nodded in agreement. "We must establish robust ethical frameworks and guidelines that govern the development and use of quantum technologies. It's of paramount importance to assess risks, mitigate potential harm, and consider the societal impact of these advancements."

Another panelist, Dr. David Thompson, a leading authority in artificial intelligence ethics, added, "With the integration of quantum computing and AI, we must address the ethical implications surrounding the use of advanced algorithms, machine learning, and data privacy. We need to strike a balance between innovation and safeguarding individual rights."

Taking these discussions to heart, Emily initiated a series of conversations within her team to address these ethical concerns. They explored topics such as data privacy, algorithmic bias, the potential for technological discrimination, and the responsible use of quantum computing's immense computational power.

Among these discussions, Dr. Elizabeth Green, a computer scientist, raised a thought-provoking question. "How do we ensure transparency and accountability in the use of quantum technologies? Should there be regulatory bodies specific to quantum applications?"

Emily considered Elizabeth's question and contemplated the potential avenues for oversight and governance. They held conversations with legal experts, policymakers, and representatives from regulatory bodies to better understand the frameworks required to ensure ethical and responsible quantum technology development.

One such conversation took place with Dr. Henry Larson, a lawyer specializing in technology policy. He emphasized the importance of striking a balance between innovation and regulation to prevent potential abuses of quantum power. "We need a forward-thinking approach to regulation," Dr. Larson said. "One that fosters innovation while safeguarding against risks, and encourages responsible development and deployment of quantum technologies."

Emily's team realized that conversations surrounding legislation, international cooperation, and consensus-building would be pivotal in shaping a responsible ecosystem around quantum technologies. They engaged with policymakers and legal scholars to discuss the development of frameworks that addressed both national and global aspects of quantum governance.

Additionally, Emily's team recognized the need to engage with society at large to ensure public awareness and democratic participation in these crucial decisions. They organized public forums, town hall meetings, and educational initiatives to foster informed discussions around the ethical implications of quantum technologies. By involving stakeholders from various backgrounds, they aimed to develop sustainable solutions that balanced societal needs and technological advancements.

Chapter 6 of the quantum revolution marked a turning point for Emily and her team. The ethical conversations they participated in exposed the importance of responsible innovation and the mitigation of potential risks. These discussions brought forth a newfound vigilance, urging them to incorporate ethical considerations into every aspect of their research and deployment of quantum technologies.

As the chapter came to an end, Emily's team emerged more committed than ever to navigate the complex realm of ethical quantum power. They understood that the responsible use of quantum technologies would play a pivotal role in shaping a future that was equitable, sustainable, and benefitted all of humanity.

Quantum Security and the Battle for Encryption

In the seventh chapter of the quantum revolution, Dr. Emily Morgan and her team delved into the critical domain of quantum security, realizing the profound impact of quantum technologies on encryption and cryptography. As quantum computers evolved, posing a potential threat to existing encryption algorithms, the race for quantum-resistant security solutions began.

Emily convened a meeting with her team, recognizing the urgency of the situation. The conversation centered around the vulnerability of current encryption methods and the need to develop post-quantum cryptographic algorithms.

"We are at a crucial point," Emily emphasized. "Quantum computers have the potential to break current cryptographic systems, making our sensitive data and communication vulnerable. It's imperative that we explore quantum-resistant solutions and forge a path towards robust encryption in the quantum era."

The team engaged in discussions with cryptographers, mathematicians, and computer scientists who specialized in post-quantum cryptography. These conversations revolved around identifying and analyzing existing encryption vulnerabilities and exploring new cryptographic protocols that could withstand attacks from quantum computers.

A notable conversation took place with Dr. Michael Roberts, a leading expert in quantum-safe cryptography. "We need to transition to encryption methods that rely on mathematical problems that are challenging even for quantum computers to solve," he explained.

Emily's team dived into the complexities of lattice-based cryptography, code-based cryptography, hash-based cryptography, and other promising post-quantum approaches. They weighed the advantages and challenges of each, evaluating their suitability for different applications and computing environments.

Simultaneously, the team recognized the need for a collaborative effort within the scientific community. This led them to establish partnerships with research institutions, industry leaders, and governmental organizations invested in quantum-safe encryption development. These collaborative conversations facilitated knowledge exchange, created research consortia, and fostered innovation in the race against time.

During a particularly insightful conversation with General Sarah Marshall, the head of a cybersecurity task force, Emily raised concerns about the potential impact of quantum computers on national security.

General Marshall acknowledged the gravity of the situation, stating, "The quantum threat extends beyond traditional encryption. Our military and intelligence agencies heavily rely on secure communication channels. We must coordinate efforts to upgrade our encryption capabilities to withstand future quantum attacks."

This discussion spurred Emily and her team to explore quantum key distribution (QKD) protocols, one of the most promising approaches to quantum security. They engaged in conversations with experts who had made significant breakthroughs in QKD, aiming to develop systems that could distribute cryptographic keys securely, even in the presence of quantum adversaries.

Furthermore, conversations surrounding the standardization and implementation of post-quantum encryption algorithms were held. Emily's team engaged with standards organizations and policymakers, highlighting the need to adopt quantum-resistant security standards and regulations on a global scale.

Chapter 7 of the quantum revolution witnessed the emergence of a global community dedicated to quantum-safe encryption. Through conversations with experts, collaboration with diverse stakeholders, and advocacy for widespread adoption, Emily and her team championed the cause of securing our digital future in the face of quantum threats.

As the chapter ended, Emily's team had made significant progress in their quest for quantum resilience. However, they also recognized that encryption was just one piece of the puzzle. Conversations surrounding quantum authentication, malware detection, and secure quantum networks would continue to shape their research and development efforts. The battle for encryption security in the quantum era had begun, and Emily's team was determined to emerge victorious.

Quantum Society and Ethical Integration

In the eighth chapter of the quantum revolution, Dr. Emily Morgan and her team turned their attention to the societal implications of quantum technologies. Quantum advancements had the potential to reshape economies, industries, and everyday life. As such, Emily sought to engage in conversations surrounding the ethical integration of quantum technologies into society.

One morning, Emily gathered her team for a brainstorming session on the ethical challenges and opportunities of quantum integration. They discussed the impact of quantum computing on traditional industries, the potential for quantum AI to automate jobs, and the need to ensure equitable access to quantum technologies.

During one conversation, Dr. Malik Singh, an economist, proposed an interesting question. "How can we ensure that quantum technologies do not exacerbate socioeconomic inequalities? And how can we promote inclusive and accessible quantum innovation?"

This question resonated deeply with the team. They recognized that conversations surrounding inclusion, accessibility, and equitable benefits from quantum technologies were essential. They engaged in discussions with stakeholders from various backgrounds, including policymakers, community leaders, and technology ethicists, to explore strategies for bridging the digital divide.

One such conversation took place with Dr. Sarah Rodriguez, a technology ethicist focusing on the societal impact of emerging technologies. She stressed the importance of engaging marginalized communities and incorporating diverse perspectives in the development and deployment of quantum technologies.

"As we build the future, we must ensure that quantum technologies are in line with ethical principles, promoting justice, fairness, and inclusivity," Dr. Rodriguez emphasized. "This involves addressing biases in algorithms, providing access to education and training, and ensuring that underrepresented groups have a voice in shaping the quantum evolution."

Inspired by these conversations, Emily's team started to advocate for educational programs that would introduce quantum science and technology to a broader audience, including students from underprivileged backgrounds. They collaborated with educational institutions and nonprofit organizations to design outreach initiatives, aiming to inspire the next generation of quantum scientists and create a more diverse quantum workforce.

Additionally, conversations surrounding data privacy and quantum technologies became crucial. The team engaged with privacy experts, legal scholars, and policymakers to explore frameworks for protecting individuals' privacy in the age of quantum computing. They sought to strike a balance between the benefits of quantum technologies and the need to safeguard sensitive information.

Dr. Emily Morgan realized that dialogue on the integration of quantum technologies should extend beyond academia and industry. It needed to reach policymakers and governmental bodies at the national and international levels. Emily engaged in conversations with representatives from various governments, discussing the development and harmonization of quantum policies and regulations to ensure responsible and ethical use of quantum technologies.

One significant conversation was held with Ambassador Maria Garcia, who was leading her country's efforts in quantum technology development. "Our policies and regulations must be forward-looking and comprehensive, fostering innovation while addressing societal concerns," Ambassador Garcia stressed. "Collaboration among nations is pivotal in establishing global ethical standards and norms for the integration of quantum technologies."

As the chapter progressed, Emily's team realized that integrating quantum technologies into society required interdisciplinary collaboration and economic transformation. They held conversations with economists, policymakers, and industry leaders to explore the potential of quantum technologies to drive sustainable development and tackle global challenges, such as climate change and healthcare.

The final pages of Chapter 8 marked a new beginning. Emily's team recognized that ethical integration and societal discussions were ongoing endeavors that needed continual engagement and adaptation. They were committed to fostering awareness, influencing policy decisions, and creating an inclusive trajectory for the quantum revolution to ensure its benefits were shared by all.

As the chapter ended, Emily's team understood that the fusion of cutting-edge technologies and ethical considerations was paramount in building a quantum society that was fair, equitable, and sustainable. They viewed their conversations and actions as catalysts for change, with the potential to shape the quantum revolution in a way that aligned with the values of humanity.

Quantum Communication and the Era of Secure Connectivity

In the ninth chapter of the quantum revolution, Dr. Emily Morgan and her team delved into the realm of quantum communication. With the rapid advancement of quantum technologies, they recognized the transformative potential of secure quantum communication, paving the way for a new era of global connectivity.

Emily assembled her team for a brainstorming session, eager to explore the opportunities and challenges associated with quantum communication. They delved into discussions about quantum teleportation, quantum entanglement, and the development of quantum networks.

One of the team members, Dr. James Reynolds, a pioneer in quantum communication, pointed out the significance of secure quantum messaging. "We have the potential to harness the power of quantum entanglement to create unbreakable cryptographic keys. This can ensure secure communication channels, immune to eavesdropping or interception," he explained.

This notion captivated the team, sparking conversations regarding the potential impact of quantum networks on various sectors such as finance, healthcare, and government communication. They recognized the need for collaboration among researchers, engineers, and policy-makers to establish protocols and standards for quantum communication infrastructure.

Through conversations with experts in the field, Emily's team explored quantum key distribution (QKD) protocols in more detail. They discussed the challenges associated with implementing QKD over long distances and the development of quantum repeaters to extend the reach of secure quantum communication.

One pivotal conversation took place with Dr. Elena Kim, a leading expert in quantum repeater technology. She explained the concept of entanglement swapping and its role in establishing long-distance quantum communication links. The team engaged in discussions, aiming to overcome technical obstacles and make significant advancements in the field of quantum repeaters.

Recognizing the need for international cooperation in quantum communication, Emily's team engaged in conversations with representatives from different countries. They advocated for the establishment of global networks and protocols to enable seamless and secure communication, overcoming geographic barriers.

Furthermore, discussions on quantum internet architectures and protocols were also held. The team sought collaboration with computer scientists and networking experts to develop hybrid quantum-classical communication systems capable of supporting a variety of applications while maintaining security and reliability.

Understanding the potential societal impact of quantum communication, Emily's team also engaged with ethicists and policymakers to explore the ethical implications surrounding the use of quantum networks. Conversations revolved around privacy concerns, data ownership, and the responsible use of quantum communication technologies.

During one particular conversation with Dr. Sophia Ramirez, the team explored how quantum communication could play a role in addressing social challenges, such as bridging the digital divide or providing secure communication in regions affected by conflicts or natural disasters. They recognized the need to ensure equitable access to quantum communication technologies, particularly in underserved communities.

As the chapter progressed, Emily's team witnessed significant advancements in the field of quantum communication. They collaborated with companies and research institutions to develop prototype quantum communication systems and test them in real-world scenarios. These experiments provided valuable insights, paving the way for further improvements and implementations.

In the closing pages of Chapter 9, Emily's team acknowledged that quantum communication was standing at the threshold of a new era. With the potential to revolutionize secure connectivity, it held the power to transform industries, enable new scientific discoveries, and connect people worldwide. They understood that the journey was far from over, as research, development, and standardization efforts would continue to shape the future of quantum communication.

As the chapter came to a close, Emily's team believed that continued collaborative efforts, multidisciplinary conversations, and ethical considerations were crucial in unlocking the full potential of quantum communication. They remained committed to ensuring that this new era of secure connectivity would benefit humanity, fostering a global network that harnessed the power of quantum technologies while upholding the values of privacy, security, and inclusivity.

The Quantum Frontier - Exploring the Unknown

In the final chapter of the quantum revolution, Dr. Emily Morgan and her team stood at the threshold of the quantum frontier, ready to embark on an awe-inspiring journey of exploration and discovery. The conversations that took place in this chapter were filled with anticipation, curiosity, and a sense of wonder as they delved into the unknown realms of quantum science.

Gathering her team one last time, Emily expressed her gratitude for their tireless efforts. "We have come a long way together," she said, her voice filled with pride. "Our conversations and collaborations have pushed the boundaries of quantum knowledge. And now, it's time to step into uncharted territory."

The conversations that followed were filled with bold ideas and daring hypotheses. Researchers, physicists, and mathematicians engaged in discussions on the nature of quantum reality, the potential of multi-dimensional quantum computing, and the exploration of exotic quantum states. Bound by their shared passion for unraveling the mysteries of the quantum world, they inspired each other to think beyond conventional boundaries.

One particularly enthralling conversation centered around the possibility of quantum time travel. Dr.

Daniel Thompson, a renowned theoretical physicist, presented his groundbreaking research on utilizing quantum entanglement to probe the fabric of time itself. The team marveled at the concept, recognizing that such a discovery could revolutionize our understanding of the universe.

Engaging in conversations with philosophers, the team also explored the philosophical implications of quantum science. They contemplated the nature of consciousness, the relationship between observer and observed, and the fundamental interconnectedness of all things. These discussions opened new avenues of thought, challenging traditional paradigms and fostering a deeper appreciation for the beauty and intricacy of the quantum world.

As Emily's team embarked on their own experimental endeavors, they engaged in collaborations with cutting-edge research facilities, exploring the potential of quantum simulations for modeling complex systems, predicting the behavior of molecules, and advancing materials science. These conversations unveiled new possibilities for solving grand challenges in areas such as climate change, drug discovery, and renewable energy.

One conversation in particular, with Dr. Victoria Chen, a pioneer in quantum materials, sparked fascination within the team. Dr. Chen explained the concept of topological quantum materials and their unique properties that could revolutionize information storage and processing. The team enthusiastically began to explore new applications for these materials, envisioning a future where quantum technology and classical computing seamlessly merged.

But beyond the scientific and technological frontiers, Emily's team also realized the importance of reflecting on the profound impact of the quantum revolution on society and humanity as a whole. They engaged in conversations with artists, writers, and visionaries who sought to capture the essence of the quantum world through their creative expressions. The fusion of science and art fueled their imagination, enabling them to envision a future where quantum-inspired creativity thrived, transcending boundaries of imagination.

In the closing pages of Chapter 10, Emily's team embarked on their individual paths, each armed with a newfound appreciation for the quantum world and a determination to explore further. They celebrated the power of conversation, collaboration, and the indomitable human spirit that had brought them to the precipice of discovery.

As the final words were written, Emily's team acknowledged that the quantum revolution was not just a scientific endeavor, but a testament to the endless human quest for knowledge and understanding. It stood as a reminder of the power of conversations to shape the course of history and transform our world.

With a beautiful finishing touch, Emily concluded, "Our journey doesn't end here. The quantum frontier stretches out before us, inviting us to push the boundaries, challenge our perceptions, and venture into the depths of the unknown. Let us continue to have conversations that ignite curiosity and drive us towards a future where the possibilities of the quantum world unfold before our very eyes."

And so, with hearts filled with hope, excitement, and a sense of awe, Emily's team stepped into the uncharted quantum frontier, ready to shape the future and leave a lasting legacy for generations to come.

About the Author

Alice Parabia

Alice Parabia is an extremely intelligent, vivacious, curious and creative girl. She has a natural knack for storytelling, story writing, topped by composing poems and songs on almost any topic. Ever since she was a little girl, she has been dreaming of writing story books and publishing them. She creates stories with her vivid imagination: weaving magic around her. She has published a book with Bribooks too called, "The doll of my dreams. She has written this book with the support of SK's Transformational Hub also known as Parivartan with her mentor Suverchala Kashyap."

www.ingramcontent.com/pod-product-compliance
Lightning Source LLC
LaVergne TN
LVHW041557070526
838199LV00046B/2027